TO770446

A **B**LACK **B**INDING **M**YSTERY

THE ENIGMA OF THE ASTRONOMER

BY **K**EITH **R**. **D**AVIS

Acknowledgement

I would like to extend my deepest gratitude to the Monuments Men & Women Foundation for their tireless efforts in preserving and restoring the world's cultural heritage. Their dedication to recovering lost masterpieces and safeguarding history ensures that future generations can continue to learn from and be inspired by these invaluable works of art. Their mission honors the bravery of those who first protected these treasures during World War II and carries it forward into the present day. Thank you for keeping the past alive and reminding us of the importance of art, history, and the stories they tell.

Book Design: Mark Jenkinson
Editor: Meghan Ziegler

DEDICATION

This book is dedicated to my family. Your love, support, and endless encouragement mean the world to me. This journey wouldn't be the same without you.

Prologue

It was the summer of 1940, and the luxurious hotel in Paris buzzed with a kind of nervous energy. Edouard Rothschild and his family found themselves in a race against time. Edouard was the director of the Bank of France, and closely involved in his family's banking and railway interests. In fact, the Rothschild name stood among the most prominent and influential families in Europe, but none of that power and influence seemed to matter in the current environment. The Jewish family had found themselves the target of a new regime in France, now under Nazi authority. In fact, the government had just ordered the confiscation of all Rothschild property, including their legendary art collection. Edouard had been able to secure safe passage to the United States for his family, but now it felt like an eternity until they could leave France and the war in Europe behind them. Their clothing trunks filled the fancy hotel suite along with several crates of their most precious artwork and possessions. They would hate for those to fall into the wrong hands, or worse, see these priceless works destroyed in an Allied invasion that would hopefully liberate the people of France some day.

Suddenly, the echo of heavy boots filled the corridor. The door to the Rothschild's suite crashed open and a group of German soldiers stormed in wearing dark uniforms with distinct red patches on their collars. An officer entered next, his face hard and emotionless as he read from a meticulously prepared list. Two soldiers moved swiftly to the corner where the crates of artwork sat. Without hesitation, they pried open the wooden lids, revealing the masterpieces within. The officer strode over to the crates as the soldiers sorted through the paintings, looking for something in particular. There was a shout of excitement as one of the soldier's found their prize. The young soldier paused for a moment, perhaps sensing the immense history and value behind the canvas as he stared at it. The officer's duty, however, overrode any appreciation for beauty. He plucked the painting from the soldier's hands, made a note on his list with cold precision, and placed it onto a waiting cart. He spun around on the tile floor as his hard heels made a sharp click and barked an order to the soldiers to box the crates back up and follow him.

Edouard and his family could only sit there huddled together and watch as the soldiers removed the crates of their priceless treasures before their eyes. The Rothschild's knew however that they were the lucky ones. At least they still had each other, which was a lot more than many other Jewish families could say these days.

PREFACE

Johannes Vermeer completed "The Astronomer" in 1688. Like many of his works, it is not very large—about 20 by 18 inches painted in oil on canvas—but there is something special about this painting. Vermeer usually painted women, like in his masterpiece "The Girl with a Pearl Earring," but this work and its companion piece, "The Geographer," are of men and focus on the ideas of knowledge and science. The men are thought to be great scholars, deep in thought about the workings of the world, not uncommon concepts in the Golden Age of Dutch painting. The Astronomer of the painting has placed his hand upon a celestial globe displaying the constellations, and as is typical of Vermeer's style, painted in such detail that you can decipher which constellations he's observing, the book he's reading, and the painting that hangs on the wall in the background. None of these details are accidental. Often the great mystery of old paintings is the who, what, and why the artist chose these things?

The painting was purchased in the late 19th century by Paris banker and art collector Alphonse Rothschild, who passed it down to his son Edouard. In 1940, the Rothschild art collection was seized by the German government during the occupation following the invasion of France. This painting, though, was at the top of a list of artwork created by Adolf Hitler himself, leading to its theft. There has always been a certain enigma surrounding "The Astronomer".

Image: Public Domain

JAMES

A fifth grader with a thirst for knowledge, a love of mysteries, and a soft spot for old books. For James, books are more than just pages and ink; they're like old friends, each with their own hidden stories waiting to be unlocked.

EMILY

Sharp-witted, pop-culture savvy, and James's best friend. At 12 years old, Emily is already a movie encyclopedia, having watched more films than most adults. Her quick memory for visuals and knack for tech make her the perfect foil to James's bookish tendencies.

GRANDPA

The heart and soul of The Black Binding, Grandpa is part master bookseller, part treasure hunter, and 100% mystery. To James, he's like an old leather-bound book: weathered and full of secrets, with many stories still waiting to be uncovered.

ELEANOR

Director of the Guardians, a group dedicated to protecting and preserving the world's most valuable artifacts and art. She's spent years uncovering lost treasures and navigating the shadowy world of stolen art. Beneath her tough exterior lies a deep passion for preserving the past.

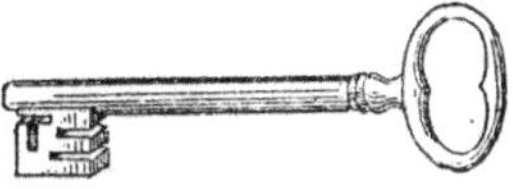

CHAPTER I

James loved old books. They were an odd thing to love for a kid his age, but then again he had also grown up among the nooks and crannies of a bookshop. Ever since he could remember, his father would tell him "There is so much to learn in a book no matter how old." Dad was funny like that.

A love of books just runs in the Hawthorne family. It helps to note that Dad is the Apprentice Bookseller at The Black Binding, a bookshop located on West Orleans Street in the "Near North" side of Chicago, IL. Chicago is a beautiful city rich in history and architectural innovation. In 1884, the Home Insurance Building soared to 10 stories high as the world's first "skyscraper". It was never considered the tallest building in the world, but the building's design approach, constructed on a steel skeleton instead of on brick and mortar, became the foundation for all future skyscraper designs.

The Adlake Building, home to The Black Binding, was originally built in 1909 to serve as the factory for the Adams & Westlake Manufacturing Company. Adams & Westlake, America's most successful railroad lantern maker, expanded to make bicycles and cameras in the early 20th century. Faded ghost signs of painted advertising can still be seen on the building's brick façade over a hundred years later. After Adams & Westlake moved out of the building, it also housed a textile manufacturer in the 1970's. Grandpa carved out his own quirky space for the bookshop years ago. Although much of the building sat vacant for years, portions of it are now renovated into office space. Inside, the high ceilings with exposed brick walls, hardwood floors, and century-old timber frame construction give the space a rustic charm and authenticity that only an old building can provide.

The eye-catching sign for The Black Binding hangs proudly above the entrance to the store, carved from dark wood, with an aura of mystery and age, hinting at the treasures hidden within the shop's walls. At the center of the sign, a large and ornately carved key is surrounded by letters reading "The Black Binding," etched in elegant script, letters standing out against dark wood, as if beckoning visitors inside to discover the shop's secrets.

The Black Binding was amazing in the way only an old bookshop could be. Like any old bookshop, it held more than books. It was a three-story paradise of unusual books and artifacts their family had collected over the years. Each level was divided into smaller rooms with enough nooks, crannies, cozy chairs, and warm corners that a person could walk into the store and not be seen by another person for hours. The small spaces and high ceilings elongated the rooms, lined with shelves of books so high a customer needed a ladder to reach the top. The ladder was usually stored in the corner.

The book shop had been in the Hawthorne family for years, opened by James's grandfather, Ben. While Grandpa was still the "Master" Bookseller, James's dad handled most of the day-to-day operations of the business.

Grandpa reminded James of an old book, with his leathery, rough and slightly wrinkled skin. In his own version of early retirement, he'd disappear among the labyrinth of rooms and books, seeing his own way out of the shop when he was ready to go. Sometimes it seemed like days between Grandpa sightings, but it was so common that often no one noticed. While he might be growing old, he had the energy of a man still in his prime and looked, James's mom said, like someone named Cary Grant. He was an actor in the 1950s and 60s. James looked him up once.

Great-Grandpa loved The Black Binding too, but he died when James was only two years old. James never got to know him well, but his parents reminded him often that his Great-Grandpa named him. Great-Grandpa was an artist and restored paintings, and fought in World War II in France and Germany as a young man. Grandpa told James that we will probably never know how much the men and women of that generation sacrificed, but that they should always be grateful. Grandpa started the bookshop because of Great-Grandpa's love of art and history, and his advice helped the shop weather the decades.

Grandpa had an eye for valuables and a fascination with obscure trinkets that set his shop apart from the average store. It was the small, but daring risks he took to obtain these items; as well as the stories of those exploits he used to entertain the customers, that kept the shop in business all these years. While his choices were odd, he just seemed to know the kind of things his customers would pay top dollar for.

Of course, it wasn't just old books. There were magazines, like Grandpa's prized collection of Saturday Evening Post's, illustrated by J.C. Leyendecker and Norman Rockwell. Shelves of Victorian crystal bottles and brass scientific equipment with big magnifying glasses lined the walls along with other antiques, paintings, and etchings sourced from all over the country and from his occasional trips to

Europe. There was a display cabinet with terrifying antique medical tools. Busts of famous composers in cast bronze and carved marble sat with glassy, colored rocks that may have been pulled from a meteor crash; these dotted the shelves and served as an occasional bookend. An iron-bound chest filled with handwritten sheet music, yellowed old documents, postcards, and letters stood next to wooden artist's easels as framed etchings leaned here and there on occasional rickety writing desks salvaged from a monastery in France.

There were animals—a collection of stuffed birds on wooden mounts ranging from tree branches to small stumps and a six foot tall black bear standing on its hind legs. James got a kick out of the bear most of all and at Christmas time decorated it with colored lights and a Santa hat. The bear stood, the single biggest thing in the corner of a wood paneled room, at the back of the ground floor which, affectionately became known as The Bear Room.

Grandpa loved keys too, and not just the one on the sign out front. He used an old skeleton key as a weight on stacks of papers. There were paintings of keys and keyholes on the walls, and occasionally, a key carved into the end of a bookshelf. There were keys on bookmarks and on trinkets at the end of the register. James asked once about the keys. Grandpa winked and said "Knowledge is the key to everything."

Chapter II

A Dutch wooden shoe, or "klomp," is a sturdy, hand-carved clog traditionally made from poplar or willow wood. With a slightly up-turned tip and hollowed interior, the shoe is designed for durability and comfort, protecting the wearer from harsh, muddy conditions. Over time, the shoe's wood takes on a weathered look, carrying the marks of both craftsmanship and everyday use in the Dutch country-side. This particular shoe is more decorative than average, and features an intricate floral carving along the toe and sides.

The shoe began its journey across oceans after being left behind in a dusty barn, forgotten with time and discovered by Grandpa during one of his visits to the Netherlands. The clog was packed alongside other European curiosities and brought back to America, making its way to his antique bookshop in Chicago, where he felt its weathered wood and intricate floral carving added a bit of curiosity and flair to the Flower Room.

Over the years, each of the small, cluttered rooms obtained a nickname based on the objects stored in there along with the books.

To go with the Bear Room, the Dog Room was lined with hundreds of framed antique prints of dogs on the walls. The Flower Room featured a flowery Victorian China tea set and a sensible matching chair. The Glass Room was filled with a collection of odd crystal bottles while the Science Room brimmed brass microscopes and big magnifying glasses.

WHY Emily remembered there was a wooden shoe in the Flower Room, she didn't know. Then again, she remembered all kinds of things like James, but with her, it was usually something visual. Emily had it tough, she had gotten braces at the end of second grade, which was really early compared to most kids, and to make things worse had just been fitted for glasses the week before. Boy did she know computers and movies though. At 12, Emily had probably seen twice as many movies as the other kids in fifth grade. She watched everything—DVDs, YouTube, independent films— and always quoted from things that James hadn't seen.

Fifth grade can be tough for some kids. For James, while school itself was easy, making friends was a lot harder. Owning the coolest book shop ever didn't mean a lot of money, and let's face it, the popular kids don't spend a lot of time in old bookshops. His clothes usually came from secondhand stores and while he really believed that there was something special about old books, he really didn't see anything special about old clothes.

That summer before fifth grade, the University of Chicago had a computer camp for kids to learn basic programming. Dad thought it would be great for James if the bookshop got a little modern technology boost. Mom thought it might be a good place for him to meet some friends. In the end, they were both right. On the first day of the class the kids separated; boys on one side, girls on the other. The instructor took one look at the room and started assigning partners and James ended up with a girl he recognized from school. She had glasses and braces, and wore a t-shirt for some rock band called Nirvana—they were popular like 30 years ago—James had looked them up.

"I didn't know they still printed those things," Emily joked when she saw James holding a copy of the programming book. "Do they hand those out at the retirement village, old man?"

James smiled "Not sure, but I think you forgot your Doc. Martens and flannel shirt to complete the 'I'm cooler than you' look." They both laughed and quickly became friends.

Emily also thought that The Black Binding was the coolest place ever, even if it was a little old fashioned. She often wondered why James would prefer to look for answers in books when it was so much easier to find out information more quickly on the internet. James, admittedly partial, thought of a book like it was a person, with its own little secrets, as all interesting people should be.

James liked to ask questions and could never be filled with enough answers. He was like a sponge for information. Every time James would ask a question about a subject to his Grandpa though, he would always give the same answer: "Did you try looking it up? The answers are all around you!"

Emily would joke back with James and Grandpa saying "You know, the answers don't have to literally be around you. There is a whole world out there!"

To which Grandpa said, again with a wink "I've seen a whole lot more of this world than you know...and you would be surprised at how much there is in this store if you know where to look."

He wasn't being mean, just trying to teach them to be resourceful. In fact, whenever James seemed to be stuck on a problem he just couldn't solve on his own, he would often find that a book would appear on his table while he wasn't looking. There would always be a red

bookmark with a gold key charm on the end sticking out of the book, and strangely enough, the bookmark rested on the page that had the answer to what he was looking for. Grandpa was funny like that.

The red bookmarks with the gold key charm were all over the Black Binding, sticking out of various books on shelves in every room. They were made of silk ribbon with what looked like a hand drawn pattern of upper and lower case letters. Grandpa must have made them himself because they weren't like the key-themed trinkets sold by the register. James figured these were to draw people's attention as they walked around the shop, kind of like the way they have "Staff Picks" at the big chain book store.

Dad loved the Black Binding and called it home. He seemed destined to become a fixture there like any of the artifacts. An old library table and antique National brass cash register served as the checkout counter at the front of the store, and Dad had his favorite spot nearby, spending most of his day by one of the big windows in a beat up leather chair reading his beloved books.

James, on the other hand, was a lot more like Grandpa and loved to wind his way in and out of the rooms, side-stepping a pile here and there his Mom was trying to organize. He loved questions and answers and the never-ending possibilities a bookshop had to offer. To him, the shop was a portal to other worlds and the exploration never ended.

Neither James or Emily was sure how this game actually started, but the Black Binding had become home to the longest running game ever played. One of them would think up a question, a place or an object, and then they would both race to see who can find it in the bookshop first. James usually went for a book, while Emily insisted antiques and artifacts were completely fair game since they were everywhere too.

This time, James ended up in the Bear Room because in addition to the giant stuffed bear it had a nice collection of books on travel and the "place" of the current challenge was Netherlands. Emily was racing to locate the wooden shoe that she remembered was in the corner of the Flower Room. James slipped around behind the stuffed bear and climbed the book shelf. On the second shelf from the top he saw a book on the Netherlands next to one about "Dutch Masters" with the distinct red bookmark, but when he went to pull the book out, the whole shelf moved. A cool breeze came from the opening behind the shelf. It was a secret passage.

Chapter III

The secret passage seemed more like a closet behind the wall, but from the little bit of light spilling in from the book shop, he could make out a string hanging from the ceiling. James reached in and pulled it, and a bare light bulb lit the little room. He was standing in front of a spiral staircase that went to another room below.

Suddenly, Emily was behind him. "What is this place?" she asked.

"There's only one way to find out!" James said excitedly. He remembered reading a book once about the Chicago Tunnel System and he quickly ran to grab it.

When James came back with the book, he started to read: "In 1889, Chicago agreed to allow the Illinois Telephone and Telegraph Company's construction of tunnels under the city to carry a network of telephone cables. Originally, the tunnels were designed to be a small passage, big enough for the cables and one maintenance person to get through. However, Chicago hadn't agreed that Illinois Telephone and Telegraph could access the construction sites through the regular manhole system. This meant that the system, 40 feet below the streets, sewers, and electric cables could only be reached at certain locations."

"Faced with few options, the company decided that a small, passenger-less railway would be able to move the large spools of telephone cable below the city. This required a bigger tunnel, revised plans, and a network of tracks, and so, the Chicago Tunnel System was born."

"The railway, it turned out, was useful to the city even after the last cable was laid. It became the go to method for moving freight, coal, and other goods through the city. By 1920, all of the old telephone cable was removed to make room for electrical wiring to and from small freight cars moving cargo along the tracks."

"A series of elevators were built throughout the city to allow

Images: © Bruce Moffat Collection.

access to the tunnel system. Five elevators were available to the public, and dozens were connected to businesses, department stores, post offices, and manufacturing companies."

James could hardly contain his excitement. Could the Black Binding have been built over one of those old elevators? The Adlake building was certainly old enough to have an access point. He turned to a page in the book with a grainy image of the tunnel map, and there was a tunnel running under Orleans Street. When James had asked

Chicago Tunnel Co. 1920s system map. © Bruce Moffat Collection.

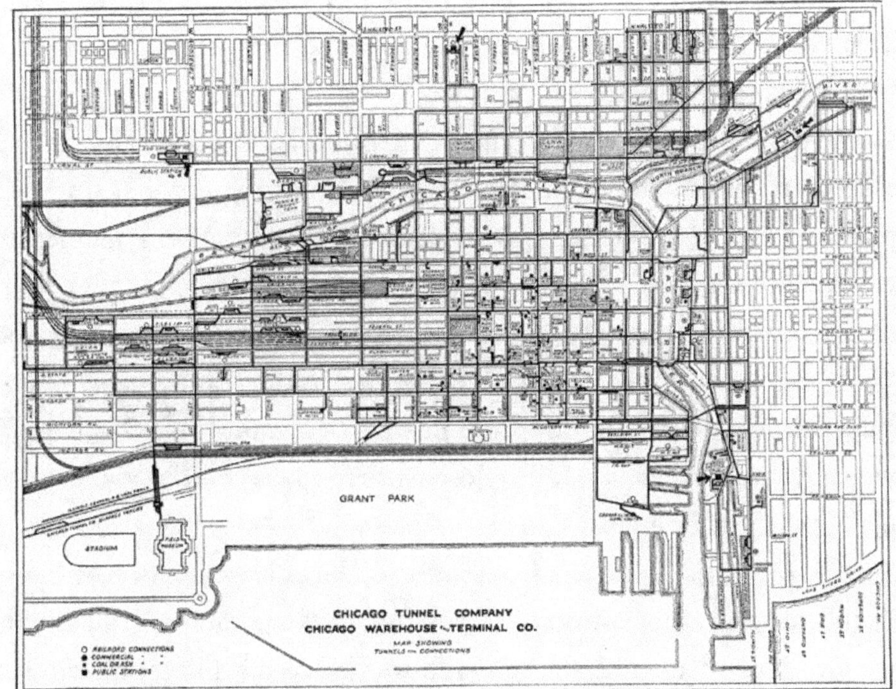

Under Every Street in the Loop and a Little Beyond

Grandpa about the tunnels, he had led James on an expedition in parts of the building to find it, but with no luck. Had Grandpa known the answer all along?

James and Emily went down the spiral staircase to a second room. It should have been the basement, but it wasn't dark and musty like the little closet above, there was something different here, a hum of electronics. Suddenly the lights came on without either of them touching a switch.

Incredibly, just underneath the old, eclectic, antique-cluttered bookshop was the most high tech room James had ever seen. The walls were covered with black and white pictures of Grandpa with Presidents Nixon, Ford, and Reagan along with a personal letter signed by George H.W. Bush during his time as CIA Director. There were some older pictures—grainy black and white photos of men in Army uniforms holding paintings, another of a young man standing in what looked like a cave with a sculpture perched on a wooden box—he looked a little like Great-Grandpa. One photo showed another group of soldiers on the steps of a castle, three holding paintings and one man standing in the center, obviously the man in charge. That picture was actually signed.

Tucked away here and there were more books. As James scanned the titles, they were unlike anything he saw in the rest of the store upstairs. Almost all of them were on European art, but there were a few books on modern art as well. There were red bookmarks sticking out of almost every one.

"Wow...this is the kind of stuff they have in sci-fi movies!" said Emily, staring at the computer screen that took up half the wall. As the two kids looked around, the screen hummed to life. "Is your Grandpa some kind of secret agent?"

CHAPTER IV

"Not exactly." said a sharp, British voice coming from a woman who suddenly appeared on the giant screen."Well this is certainly a situation, James." she said.

She had an air of no-nonsense about her and James got the feeling that she was someone very important. James sensed that his whole life was about to change.

Her hair was graying, short, neatly cut and parted on the side. She wore dark-framed glasses with small rectangular lenses that perched high on her nose, and a nicely tailored black suit with a long jacket.

She studied him closely. "You didn't ask how I knew your name." She lifted an eyebrow. It felt like James was being interviewed.

James figured he should say something. "My guess would be that if Grandpa had this secret room, he probably works for some kind of secret government organization, and you guys already know everything about everyone and their families."

"I knew it!" cried Emily. "You track our every move, don't you? I probably have a microchip in my back somewhere, don't I?"

The woman chuckled. "If it were that easy, most of us would be out of a job. Although, I'm glad to see that rumor is still out there. It helps keep some people in line."

"Honestly, I expected better of you James. Your grandfather speaks so highly of your gift." James closed his eyes and thought hard. (He always did his best thinking with his eyes closed). Sometimes, he felt like he could put a whole puzzle together in his head. All the pieces were there, a mosaic of mental pictures: things he'd read, things he'd seen, all there behind his closed eyes. They just had to be rearranged. Remove the clutter...focus on the puzzle.

Emily grinned at the small woman on the screen. "Wait until you see this!"

James opened his eyes, excited. Nothing made him happier than figuring something out. "Grandpa's like an artifact hunter. I might know why my Great-Grandpa named me James." A few years back, Grandpa gave James Robert Edsel's book, "The Monuments Men". Before Emily could pull out her phone to search online, James continued. "During World War II, the fighting in Europe threatened the safety of some of the world's greatest artworks. Paintings, sculptures, books, and some of the greatest examples of architecture known to man were destroyed daily by bombs and warfare."

"Adolf Hitler, created a special group tasked with stealing great works of art to display in Hitler's personal collection and with destroying art he felt was unworthy. Almost five million items were either stolen, hidden, or destroyed in Europe during World War II."

"Very good, James," the woman replied, nodding. "Because of this destruction, President Roosevelt established the Roberts Commission in 1943 to preserve cultural architecture and artifacts in war-torn areas. The members of the Monuments, Fine Arts, and Archives program, or MFAA, were given the nickname the Monuments Men."

"They were a small group of members present on the front lines of battles all over Europe to assist the Army with strategic positions and to prevent damage to important historic sites. They were key in the recovery of millions of artifacts, sculptures, paintings, even gold stolen by the Nazisn. It became known as 'The Greatest Treasure Hunt in History'."

A smile crept to the corners of the woman's mouth. "You know, you remind me of your great-grandfather a bit."

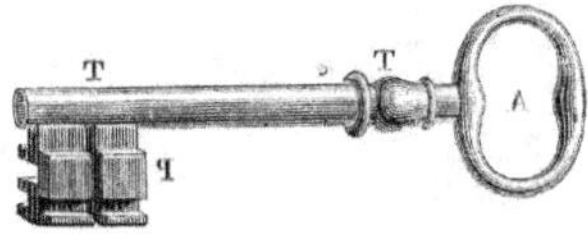

Chapter V

"That's him in this photograph, isn't it?" James asked, pointing at the grainy photograph of the young man in the cave with the sculpture. "This one too, on the steps of the castle, and the man who signed it, the one in the middle..that's James Rorimer. Is that who he named me after?"

"Yes, your great-grandfather always idolized James, and for good reason." She said.

The picture on the castle steps was actually taken at Neuschwanstein Castle, the "fairy tale" castle perched on a rocky hill in Germany so picturesque, it served as Walt Disney's inspiration for Sleeping Beauty's Castle at Disneyland. Lesser known however, was that this marvelous structure was one of the largest storage locations of stolen artwork from both the Louvre in Paris, and some of the richest and most influential families in France. James Rorimer, an American, in fact, the youngest curator of medieval art at the Metropolitan Museum of Art in New York City, was the Monuments Man who ultimately followed the trail of clues that led his team to this incredible recovery.

Images: National Archives and Records Administration, College Park, MD / Public Domain

He was aided greatly by the fearless Rose Valland, a woman from the French Resistance in Nazi occupied Paris. She retained her position as overseer of the Jeu de Paume Museum, which was used by the ERR as the temporary storage and sorting depot for all the looted artwork in France. For four years, she observed and personally noted information on over 20,000 pieces of artwork in hidden notebooks. She pretended to speak only French while secretly knowing German fluently, spying on the Nazi's conversations and memorizing their meticulous records, so that she could record the information when she got home each night. She hoped that one day, the Allies would arrive to liberate Paris. Then maybe, just maybe she would find someone to share all her knowledge to and restore the treasures of France back to their rightful owners.

Image: Archives des Musées Nationaux

James Rorimer had an incredible journey through Europe, landing in Normandy on the heels of the D-Day invasion and working his way to Paris through war-ravaged towns. With no funding, men or commanding rank to exert authority, he and the other Monuments Men had to rely on their quick-thinking and resourcefulness to get an important job accomplished in the middle of a World War. Along the way, he evaluated centuries-old churches and cultural sites, damaged public art and sculptures both cataloging and attempting to preserve what he could for future generations.

Arriving in Paris after its liberation by Allied forces, Rorimer worked hard to earn the trust and respect of Valland, who was understandably fearful of turning over her life's work to the wrong person. It was only after he showed his level of character and genuine concern for the cultural heritage of France, and not just the Army that he truly earned her trust.

That same trust and confidence he earned from Rose Valland was earned from others as well. He quickly rose in rank and in-turn was able to assemble a team of MFAA soldiers to aid the recovery of France's cultural treasures and follow the trail of clues from one storage location to the next until he ultimately reached Neuschwanstein Castle. It took two months working around the clock to remove all the stolen artwork hoarded in every room of the castle. The only ones allowed inside until the work was completed were Rorimer and his team.

One of these MFAA soldiers was a young private from Chicago who studied Art History and Painting. James had never really put the pieces together that his great-grandfather might be a real hero. He had enlisted in the Army like many of his friends, but was recruited to the Monuments Men because of his skills and knowledge. He helped restore and preserve damaged paintings and sculptures in some of

France's oldest churches until he was assigned to Rorimer's team. After the war, he returned to Chicago and started a family, but the job was never really done. Nearly two million cultural artifacts have yet to be recovered decades later, including famous lost works by Vermeer, Rembrandt, Picasso, Raphael and others.

The woman spoke again "Just recently, an old man in Berlin, Germany was found to have hidden 300 stolen works of art for 60 years in his apartment. There are more hiding places and people like him out there. Your great-grandfather did, and your grandfather is still doing a service to his country and the people of the world robbed of their possessions and heritage all these years later. It certainly is something to be proud of James."

Chapter VI

James could picture his great-grandfather in his olive-drab uniform and little round glasses, poring over a battered Moleskine journal, taking notes and photographs, knee-deep in the ruined rubble of the wall of a 500-year-old church. What a job it must have been for him and the others—trying to preserve more than a thousand years of culture in the middle of the war that changed the world.

The woman must have read his mind "It must have been a fascinating and lonely challenge; the Monuments Men worked alone, assigned to an Army division, but not part of a typical unit. Most of them were older, educated, established professionals, like architects, museum curators, historians, conservators, and educators. They all believed that the duty of cultural preservation was worth the risk of service in a war-torn landscape."

She continued, "The demands of the upper class worlds they left behind prepared them for this assignment in a way other soldiers could not. High, educated society requires a level of tenacity and the ability to recognize opportunity in order to get ahead. They needed

to be organized, quick thinking, and willing to improvise to achieve their goals."

Theirs was a different form of valor than that of the brave soldiers who fought across the continent and liberated its people; but for the Europeans, who value art, sculpture, and architecture, as much a part of their culture as the people themselves, it was a worthwhile fight.

"Who do you work for?" James asked "I'm assuming it's not the Monuments Men, since you don't look like the Army."

"Not anymore." she chuckled. "My name is Eleanor Chase. I am the director of a team we call the Guardians. We operate outside government control to protect and restore cultural artifacts, a process started by the Monuments Men. We are funded by philanthropists, art collectors, and other like-minded groups. This gives us, and experts like your grandfather, the means and methods to carry out our missions."

"Missions?" Emily gasped. "That sounds so cool!"

"Yes." Eleanor nodded. "Acquiring and restoring stolen artifacts can be pretty cool, and also pretty difficult. There is a lot of opposition by some pretty nefarious groups."

"What, like evil collectors?" Emily was practically hyperventilating at this point "Big, shadow organizations and rogue art dealers? Rich guys with secret stolen art collections?" she joked.

"That's exactly it." said Eleanor. "There is an organized group we unfortunately see quite a bit. They are known as the Obscura, and they work in secret by manipulating auctions, and even government regulations to acquire lost or stolen masterpieces. They are motivated only by their greed, providing black market dealers and private collectors access to priceless paintings and artifacts from all over the world. If they could, they would erase the artifact's past entirely, making it impossible for the world to know what was stolen or, in fact, that anything was stolen at all—to them, our human history is something that can be bought and sold."

James jumped in. "I've heard that many of the famous paintings you see in museums are actually fakes. My grandfather told me that Edvard Munch's "The Scream" was stolen from a museum in Norway a long time ago. The painting was returned, but the rumor is that it's a forgery and the real one is long gone."

Eleanor grimaced. "Speaking of your grandfather, have you seen him lately? I'm starting to get concerned."

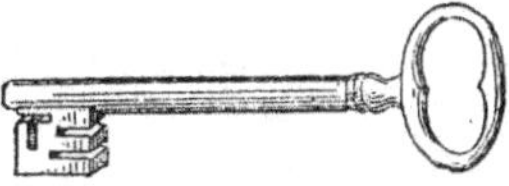

CHAPTER VII

James started pacing. It had been two days since he'd seen Grandpa. Normally, he'd just assume Grandpa had vanished into the stacks to work on one of his projects, but now the silence was deafening. Each moment felt like an eternity.

Eleanor brought up a painting on the screen. It was of a man sitting at a table under a window, surrounded by books and other scientific instruments, his hand resting on some sort of celestial globe. James marveled at the light in the painting—the way it streamed in from the window as if its presence in the room was as important as the man. "Have you ever seen this painting?" she asked.

"No" said Emily. James wasn't sure he recognized it either.

"This painting is Johannes Vermeer's 'The Astronomer'. Vermeer was a Dutch Master from the 16th century, and it's a priceless work of art with a very complicated history." Eleanor told them about the Rothschilds and how the painting was seized in 1940 for Adolf Hitler's personal collection at his request. "It was supposed to be the crown jewel of his Fuhrer-Museum in Linz, his Austrian hometown after the war. You see, Hitler had dreams of turning Linz into a modern day Florence—the great artistic and cultural center of Europe with his Fuhrer-Museum in the center, containing all the greatest works in the world. He had a scale model of the planned museum built in his secret bunker. He was obsessed with this idea, and had a special group tasked with seizing all the art on his list."

She continued, bringing up another grainy photograph of two soldiers holding up the Vermeer piece, surrounded by stacks of other paintings. "This was a salt mine in Altaussee, one of the other major storage sites for art stolen by the Nazis. It was discovered after the their surrender in 1945 and held almost 6500 paintings, including this one by Vermeer, others by Rembrandt, and a priceless marble sculpture by Michelangelo called 'The Bruges Madonna'."

Eventually "'The Astronomer' was returned to the Rothschilds, and upon Guy Rothschild's death in 1982, it was donated to the Louvre in Paris where it hangs to this day. Or does it?"

Eleanor continued. "Your grandpa shared some disturbing news with me during our last conversation. He found evidence that the Vermeer in the Louvre is a forgery, and he was on the trail of the real 'Astronomer', rumored to be held in an Obscura storehouse somewhere in the network of Chicago's underground tunnels. The last thing he told me was that he was heading down to investigate, and he would send me the location of the storehouse when he found it."

James shivered. The Obscura, a shadowy organization reaching into every corner of the city, existed and now, Grandpa may have fallen into their clutches!

Eleanor said urgently "James, your grandpa would have left behind clues, but he must have been careful in case the Obscura ever found this place. He is a bit of an enigma. He uses that word quite a bit, doesn't he?"

James frowned, a flicker of uncertainty crossing his face as he considered the task ahead. "How will I find these clues?" he asked.

Eleanor's response was swift and unwavering. "Trust in yourself, James," she said, her words encouraging him. "Your grandfather believed in you, and I'm sure he believed that you could unravel his mysteries. The key has to be somewhere in the bookshop."

Emily rolled her eyes sarcastically as she thought of all the shelves of books, rooms and nooks of the Black Binding, "A lot of good that will do. There are keys all over the bookshop!"

Image: Public Domain

CHAPTER VIII

"Keys. Keys. Keys. Grandpa's keys..." James muttered, thinking. Suddenly, he thought of Grandpa's red bookmarks—the ones with the gold key charm. "Maybe it IS the keys!" He could picture one in his head. "Emily, isn't there one on the bookshelf in the Bear Room?" Emily ran back upstairs to grab it.

A minute later she came down with the book. "It's even in a book about Dutch Masters. Seems like a clue to me." She opened the book. An old, handwritten receipt fell out and landed on the floor. Emily picked it up and scrunched up her face trying to read it. "It looks like a receipt from the bookshop, but every line is some sort of gibberish. This HAS to be a code! How do we break it?"

James closed his eyes again, thinking back to Eleanor describing his grandpa as an enigma. She was right; he used that word a lot. There was something about the way his grandpa used the word "enigma" that he just couldn't get out of his head. "Enigma," he said out loud. "Where have I heard that before?"

"Isn't that the name of 'the Riddler' in Batman? Edward Nigma...E. Nigma?" Emily said.

Eleanor chimed in. "The Enigma machine? The German code cipher device from World War II. I'll have you know a British team broke that code!"

"That's it!" said James. "It's got to be it!" The Enigma machine was a marvel of German engineering and cryptography, and was invented in the years leading up to World War II. It was designed as a secure method of communication for businesses and government, but its potential for military applications was obvious. By the late 1920s, the German military started using the Enigma as its encryption device.

Eleanor continued "The Enigma's intricate system of rotors scrambled plain text messages into ciphertext, making them virtually impossible to decipher. Throughout the war, German forces relied heavily on the Enigma for secure communication, believing its encryption to be unbreakable. However, an Allied team..." Eleanor gave a little bow "...most notably those at Britain's Code and Cypher School, built their own machine to decipher Enigma-encoded messages. They basically built the first computer—the Turing Computer—named after its inventor Alan Turing."

"Successfully breaking the Enigma code played a crucial role in Allied victory and provided valuable intelligence on German military movements. Breaking the Enigma code remains one of the greatest achievements in the history of cryptography, forever altering the course of World War II and shaping the future of modern computing. You don't think your grandfather has an Enigma machine in his store, do you?"

Emily laughed. "Have you seen this place? If there's one in Chicago, it's around here somewhere." She pulled out her phone and did an image search for "Enigma machine". "Okay. It looks like a wooden box on the outside with an old-timey typewriter inside it. There are three gears at the top which must be the rotors you talked about, and a bunch of letters above the typewriter keys."

"It was the rotors that really scrambled the code though." James said, remembering one of his talks with Grandpa. "Three Rotors, each with the 26 letters of the alphabet that you could set to a certain combination. Those three letters could create thousands of combinations, and then the wiring inside the machine scrambled the letters a second time. Some machines had a set of plugs on the bottom that could scramble the code a third time! Someone would need to know all three of the settings to properly break a code."

"Well, let's get searching!" cried Emily. "There's a dusty wooden box out there with our name on it!"

Image: Public Domain

Chapter IX

Eleanor called after them. "Let me know if you find it!" But the kids were already gone.

They raced through the labyrinth of shelves in the Black Binding, their eyes scanning nooks and crannies for any clue about the location of the Enigma machine. The air hung thick with the scent of old books and dust. Something was nagging James. He'd seen this machine before, but he just couldn't bring the memory to the front of his mind.

As they searched around the Science Room, Emily whistled. She'd spotted a weathered wooden box tucked away on a low shelf, underneath a table crowded with brass equipment and magnifying glasses.

James peered over her shoulder, his breath catching as he caught sight of it nestled amidst the artifacts. "This must be it," James whispered, his voice barely audible in the hushed confines of the bookshop. "Grandpa hid it right here, in plain sight!"

They struggled to lift the heavy machine out from its hiding place. They set it on a small table and stared. This humble wooden box could be the key to not just solving a big mystery, but opening the doors to many more. James lifted the lid silently. It was unmistakable. It looked just like the picture Emily found, with black typewriter keyboard, three rows of lamp letters, and the three dials at the top to turn the rotors to a 3-letter key. "So now what?" Emily said.

James ran back to get the Dutch Masters book and the old book store receipt with the code written on it. The red bookmark, complete with gold key charm, fell out onto the table. "First, we need to set the rotors to a three letter key."

"But that could be anything!" Emily said, "How would we know what three letters to use?"

James glanced down at the red bookmark and the pattern of handwritten letters. Most of the nonsense words were a string of lowercase letters but only three of the letters on the bookmark were capitalized. "Let's try 'H V E' to start."

Emily set the dials on the rotors. "Now what?"

James pulled out the receipt and handed it to Emily. He grabbed a piece of scrap paper and a pencil. "Now type in the letters from the receipt and the unscrambled letters should light up above them. I'll write them down."

Emily deliberately started to type the letters as James wrote:

FOUND VERMEER ASTRONOMER
OBSCURA AUCTION, MAY 10
STOREHOUSE NEAR TUNNEL STATION 2
MONTGOMERY WARD

"The old Montgomery Ward building? That's only a few blocks away!" said Emily as she looked it up on her phone. As they ran back down to Grandpa's secret office to tell Eleanor, she started reading from the History of Chicago website.

Emily continued, "Montgomery Ward was the first mail order catalog business in the United States. The large Mail Order House covered more than two million square feet along the North Branch of the Chicago River with literal miles of chutes, elevators, and a shipping platform big enough to hold 24 railroad freight cars. The 8-story Administration Building across the street served as the company headquarters. They were the first cast-in-place concrete structures in Chicago, the pioneers of a new 20th century construction technique for construction. A four story tower complete with pyramid roof was added to the building in 1929, with a bronze statue atop the pyramid named 'The Spirit of Progress.' The statue represented the goddess Diana balanced on a globe, holding a torch in one hand and a caduceus in the other. Both buildings have since been converted into high-end apartment complexes."

"Montgomery Ward was a major station in the Chicago Tunnel System, 40 feet below the street." James told Eleanor as he looked through his book. "This must be where the Obscura storehouse is located. I bet Grandpa was trying to get there through the tunnels!"

"May 10. Two days away," mused Eleanor. "and our agent on the ground, your grandfather..." she looked toward James, concerned. "...has gone missing!"

CHAPTER X

"We've got to find him!" James said, starting for the door. "What are we waiting for?"

"I agree." Eleanor began. "However, you two can't just go running off by yourselves. I can have an agent at Montgomery Ward by tonight. We can't have anything happen to you in the meantime, so stay put and let us handle it!"

"But..." interrupted Emily.

"Absolutely not!" Eleanor insisted forcefully, then softened. "I know how concerned you are, but I promise we will be in touch the minute we have news. You have already done so much to help and for that we are grateful. Now, I must go. Promise me that you will stay where you are." The screen went black. James and Emily stared at it for a moment, then at each other, speechless.

Emily spoke first. "Well, we're obviously not just going to sit here and do nothing. So what's the plan?"

James smiled. "I've already got one! Let's meet back here in an hour. Bring a flashlight and a backpack. I'll dig up a map of the tunnel system that's not in the book." He couldn't bear to tear a page out of a book. "I'm sure it's around here somewhere. I'll also try to find the access point to the tunnel in the basement."

Emily ran out of the room while James finally took a good look around Grandpa's secret room.

He stared at the pictures on the wall, then scanned the titles of the books on the shelves. There were stacks of paper and more books on the floor. On a small writing table, he saw another book about the Chicago Tunnel System, a folded sheet of paper sticking out of the pages. There it was! The map!

James found a compass and changed into a new t-shirt and jeans for the journey underground. He headed down to the basement to find the tunnel access point.

It had to be there. When Grandpa led James on their little expeditions, he never let him explore the north corner of the building. The cool, musty air greeted him as he descended the creaky wooden stairs, his flashlight casting long shadows on the stone walls. James's heart raced as he approached the north corner, the beam of his flashlight revealing old boxes stacked haphazardly against the wall. Surprisingly, the boxes were completely empty and moved aside as easily as if they were a false wall. There in the corner of the basement, behind the wall of boxes, was an old coal elevator, a sign of the building's industrial past and the access point to the Tunnel System below. Its iron frame was darkened by years of soot and its old paint flaked off in patches, revealing the reddish-brown iron beneath.

The elevator was a sturdy, open box-like structure made of metal I-beams. Thick cables hung on either side, attached to the massive gears above powering the lift. The wooden slats of the elevator's floor were smooth from decades of coal dust and grime. A small, weathered control panel with a single lever operated its up and down motion.

Emily arrived with a flashlight and a leather backpack as James took in the elevator. "You mean this old death trap is how your Grandpa got into the tunnels? He's braver than I thought!"

James got out the map and his compass. The map showed the streets of Chicago laid out in a grid, with bold dark lines highlighting the Tunnel System 40 feet below the streets. "Orleans Street runs north/south and Montgomery Ward is about three blocks west and then about five blocks north once we hit the river. If we keep the compass and Orleans Street on the map pointing north and head west through the tunnels under Ohio Street we should be going the right direction."

The two kids stepped onto the worn wooden platform and James put his hand on the lever. "Let's go find Grandpa!" He pulled the lever and the old gears above began to lower the platform down.

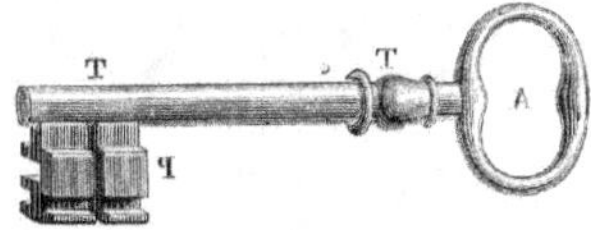

CHAPTER XI

The elevator moved slowly but smoothly. Grandpa must have greased the gears and kept it in working condition over the years. It reached the bottom of the shaft with a thud and they were in complete darkness. A cool, stale breeze brushed across their faces and they switched on their flashlights. The tunnel was egg shaped and just wide enough for them to stand side-by-side. James took out the map and compass and oriented it north. "It looks like we are going this way," he said, pointing down the tunnel to the west. The light from their flashlights danced off the walls as they worked their way along the tunnel. They could still see faint lines on the ground of the old railroad tracks where cars ran beneath the streets all those years ago.

James followed the map, looking along the path and counting the tunnels that branched off either side as they walked. They walked straight until the tunnel they were in started to angle to the right. "We must be near the river," James said. "It shouldn't be far, just a few more blocks until we reach the Montgomery Ward tunnel station."

In 1992, workers repairing the Kinzie Street Bridge accidentally

damaged a wall of the Tunnel System, and the Chicago River above started flooding the tunnels with millions of gallons of water, even filling the basements of some old buildings. James swallowed nervously. It would not be a good time for that to happen again! They worked their way north a few more minutes until they reached a large opening that seemed like a cavern compared to the small, egg-shaped tunnel, even if the ceiling was still low and cramped. "This must be the station beneath Chicago Avenue. The warehouse is to the north and the old Montgomery Ward headquarters is to the south."

They scanned the walls of the underground station. "Which way should we go?" said Emily. "I think there might be something on the warehouse side, don't you?"

"I think so too," agreed James "There should be a large lift below the warehouse where they would lower loads from the train line above. That will probably be our best way up." They crept along the walls in case they weren't alone, but the old underground station was deserted. They found the same boxy steel beam elevator structure they'd found in the bookshop's basement, but this one was definitely larger than that small coal lift. Emily took a deep breath and pulled the lever. The lift started to go up.

Their hearts were in their throats as they listened to the gears squeak above, much louder than the ones Grandpa maintained. James imagined a group of burly henchmen waiting for them when they reached the top, but the lift came to a stop and all was silent here, too. Had he been wrong about Grandpa's message? Was any of this real, or is it something they just made up after too much boredom in the store?

This railyard was larger than the station below, with high ceilings and a cool, fresh breeze from the abandoned entrances at each end where the old train cars entered. Moonlight streamed through broken windows, illuminating the walls around them so well they could turn off their flashlights to avoid detection. They moved quickly but silently, senses alert for any hint of movement or sound. Suddenly, James stopped, reaching out a hand to stop Emily. Ahead, a faint orange glow seeped through a narrow crack beneath a door in the storehouse, illuminating the dust on the ground. His heart racing, James crept closer, peering through the old keyhole.

Inside, shadows danced across the walls of a large stone walled room filled with crates and ancient artifacts. In the center in a dim pool of light sat Grandpa, tied to a chair, his eyes scanning the room with determination. "We found him!" James breathed, relief washing over him.

Emily nodded, eyes wide with fear. "How do we get in?" she whispered. James scanned the area, looking for any sign of movement inside the room. It seemed like Grandpa was alone. With a careful hand, he turned the old doorknob, opening a gap just large enough for them to squeeze through.

"One at a time." James whispered, motioning for Emily to go first. She slipped through the opening like a shadow, moving soundlessly on the other side. James followed, trying to not make a sound. They crept closer to Grandpa, who met their eyes with a silent urgency but also complete shock that these two kids were standing in front of him.

"Quietly," Grandpa mouthed, straining against his bonds. As they worked to free him, the distant shuffle of footsteps echoed through the chamber. James and Emily froze. They were not alone. "Hide... over there!" Grandpa whispered, tilting his head to the left at a gap between two crates. The two kids scurried over and squeezed in just as a heavyset man in thick-soled shoes came stomping into the room.

CHAPTER XII

"Just checking that you're still alive in here, pops." the man growled. "We thought we heard some noises in here from the warehouse. Not getting any funny ideas, are ya?"

Grandpa leaned back in the chair, not betraying anything about the plan. James was amazed at how cool and calm he looked. "Now where would I be going at this point, Vince...besides, you have done so much to make me comfortable." Which was obviously an attempt at a joke since being tied to a hard wooden chair was hardly a luxurious way to spend the past day.

The guard gave a chuckle. "You're a crafty old man, I'll give you that. I'm not putting anything past you." He paused, and added "Won't be long now, so just stay put and let the deal happen. I'd hate to see anything happen to your family and that old bookshop."

As the men talked, James scanned the crates and shelves around the walls. There were paintings and sculptures, big and small; some he recognized, but others he had never seen before. Could these all be real? Was Eleanor right? Had the Obscura been dealing in stolen artwork and replacing paintings hanging in museums around the world with copies? It sure seemed like it, and that would mean that Grandpa really WAS an agent for the Guardians too. They had to rescue him, but James had a feeling that Grandpa wasn't leaving without "The Astronomer" either.

Vince started to leave, then turned. "Just sit right there," he said. "It'll all be over soon."

James listened to the heavy sounds of the guard's footsteps fading away until he heard a door open and close. James and Emily crept back out from between the crates and hurried over to Grandpa to untie him.

"Where is 'The Astronomer'?" James asked Grandpa as they loosened his ropes. "Eleanor said she could have an agent here by tonight, but we wanted to find you as soon as possible."

Grandpa looked at James and Emily with pride. "You met Eleanor? I knew you two were smart, but I can't believe you actually figured it all out! So you found the Enigma and deciphered the code?"

"Yeah, we did." said Emily, "Look how much stuff they have in here. This is amazing!"

Grandpa stood up, massaged his wrists, and stretched his legs. "It's a lot bigger than even I knew. This is only one storehouse. There are others in the country, and more around the world," he explained. "'The Astronomer' is just the tip of the iceberg." As they started to look around the room, James started to understand what Grandpa meant. There were hundreds of works of art all around them, and this was only one storehouse!

Near the door Vince used to leave the room, James saw it. It was smaller than he had imagined it, but with an unearthly glow about it—a signature of Vermeer's work. The painting sat on top of a crate,

leaned against the wall. There was no frame around it, just a canvas stretched over a wooden frame.

Grandpa walked toward it. "There is one way to check and then we will know for sure." He picked up the painting and turned it over. There, in black ink, was stamped a swastika, the unmistakable symbol of the Nazi party. "In 1940, when the Hitler's forces seized this painting, it was destined for Adolf Hitler himself. This painting was to be the crown jewel of his collection."

Emily took off her backpack. "You can put it in here." she offered. Grandpa carefully slipped the painting into her backpack. She slid it back on her shoulders.

"We better get out of here," Grandpa said. "The auction is in two days and they will want to come get the painting soon."

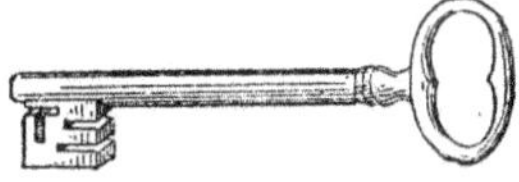

CHAPTER XIII

As they edged toward the exit of the storehouse, Emily clutched her arms close to the straps on the backpack holding the priceless painting. James kept a firm grip on Grandpa, who was still weak from being held prisoner.

The silence was shattered by footsteps clattering in the hallway outside. The door crashed open and Vince burst in, followed by a tall, imposing man with a sharp gaze and neatly tailored gray suit. He had a vivid blue tie and a dark gray wool trench coat. As he stepped into view, he was followed by two more burly guards. This must be the Obscura leader.

"Well, well," he sneered, his voice dripping with arrogance. "I see the family reunion is complete. But I'm afraid you won't be leaving with that painting. There is far too much resting on this auction and I won't have it ruined by some old man and a couple of kids."

Emily's voice was shaky as she whispered to James. "We need to distract them."

James nodded, his mind racing. He glanced around the room, spotting a stack of crates nearby. Without a second thought, he pushed the stack over, sending them loudly crashing to the ground. The noise reverberated through the storehouse, momentarily catching the henchmen off guard.

"Run!" Grandpa urged, his voice hoarse but determined. They sprinted toward the door, weaving between stacked crates, jumping over a Greek marble bust and dodging a large blue & white Ming Vase.

The Obscura weren't far behind. The leader barked orders to his men to seize them, but not harm the painting. The sound of heavy footsteps echoed behind them, growing louder with each passing second. The kids and Grandpa crashed through the door out into the railyard, moonlight streaming through the old windows. James led the way, his eyes scanning for any possible escape route. If they could get back to the lift, perhaps they can escape back down into the underground tunnels. "This way!" he shouted, guiding Emily and Grandpa in the right direction.

As they reached the old iron elevator, the men closed in, blocking their path.

"There's no escape," the leader growled, drawing a pistol from beneath his trench coat. Emily let out a defeated sigh, but James refused to give up. He stood behind Emily, shielding the backpack with his body.

Grandpa stepped in front of both kids "You'll have to go through me to get it," he said, his voice trembling.

The man with the blue tie raised his gun, a twisted smile on his face. "That can be arranged," he said, tightening his finger on the trigger.

A sudden shout echoed through the railyard. "FBI...drop your weapon!" Flashlights blazed to life around them. They were surround-

ed by a group of FBI agents, their own guns trained on the man in the blue tie and his henchmen while the red and blue lights of the Chicago Police swirled outside. The leader hesitated, glancing between his men and the law. For a brief moment, he seemed to consider his options, but it was clear he was outnumbered.

With a snarl, he lowered his weapon, signaling for his men to do the same. "This isn't over," he spat. The FBI quickly moved in, disarming the men and securing the area. James, Emily, and Grandpa breathed a collective sigh of relief as the tension finally broke.

An FBI agent turned to face Grandpa. "Our office got notification from Eleanor Chase that you might be here. I have her on the phone now." She turned her phone toward the three heroes and Eleanor's face glowed back at them. The smile on her previously stern face was ear to ear.

Emily spoke first. "When you said you could have an agent here, this is not what I expected!"

Eleanor laughed. "Well, you might not know this, but the FBI has a program that tracks and investigates art theft and illegal sales. It's our first call when we get a lead." She looked at James, who handed the Vermeer to the agent, who carefully inspected the canvas. "You did it!" Eleanor said, her voice filled with admiration. "You saved a priceless piece of history."

As they prepared to leave the railyard, James glanced back at the Obscura leader, now in handcuffs. "He's right about one thing though," James said quietly. "This isn't over. There's still so much out there we don't know about."

The FBI agent nodded in agreement. "At least we're on the right path. There is an awful lot of artwork here that can finally get back to its rightful owners. You all did a great job tonight."

With the Vermeer safe in the hands of the FBI, the two kids and

Grandpa were escorted home to The Black Binding. It was quite an ordeal, but they had done it—they had saved Grandpa, recovered the painting, and thwarted the Obscura's plans. As they stepped out of the car outside the bookshop, James couldn't help but feel a sense of pride. They had faced incredible danger and come out stronger on the other side. And though the journey was far from over, they knew they could face whatever came next—together.

CHAPTER XIV

The next day in The Black Binding, the warm glow of the old lamps still cast a comforting light over the familiar shelves, but the shop felt a lot smaller to James. The scent of aged paper and dusty antiques filled the air—a big change from the cold, damp tunnels they had just explored the night before. James and Emily sat in overstuffed chairs in the center of the Dog Room talking excitedly about their adventure. Suddenly, they heard a knock on the door and turned to see Grandpa standing there. He still seemed weary from his time in captivity, but he was starting to look more like his old self again. "You kids have a visitor," he said with a little twinkle in his eye.

Grandpa stepped aside. There stood Eleanor herself, having traveled all the way from London. She stared at the two kids for a moment and then her stern expression gave way to a smile. "You both did incredibly well," she finally said, her voice filled with pride. "You were brave, resourceful...and a little disobedient... everything the Guardians stand for."

James looked up, his face full of questions. "Grandpa... Eleanor... what, I mean who exactly are the Guardians?"

Eleanor exchanged a glance with Grandpa before sitting down across from the kids. "The Guardians are a group dedicated to protecting and preserving the world's most valuable artifacts and art," she explained. "We've been working against the Obscura for years, and we knew this time they were after something big."

"Like 'The Astronomer'!" Emily said, nodding toward Grandpa. "He was trying to find the real Vermeer before they could sell it."

Grandpa nodded. "Exactly, but 'The Astronomer' was just the tip of the iceberg. The Obscura dabble in all sorts of illegal activities, from art theft to artifact smuggling. Until now, we've only been able to stop them piece by piece."

"All that changed last night. Now you're a part of this too." Eleanor added, looking at James and Emily with a serious expression. "You've proven you can handle the danger, but it's not something we take lightly. If you're going to continue down this path, you need to understand the risks."

James stood, determined. "Of course we want to help. This is bigger than just us—it's about protecting history, about doing what's right." Then he looked at Grandpa and smiled proudly. "It's what my family does."

Emily nodded in agreement. "I mean, we can't just go back to pretending everything's normal. We've seen too much."

Grandpa smiled back, a mix of pride and concern in his eyes. "I knew you'd say that, but let's take it one step at a time. For now, let's focus on keeping the bookshop running and staying out of sight. They may know where we are, but they also know that we'll be ready."

As the night wore on, their conversations shifted from the immediate dangers to the future. Eleanor and Grandpa made plans to reinforce the Black Binding's defenses, to research what he overheard about the Obscura's activities while being captured, and to train the kids in the skills they'd need for the challenges ahead.

For now though, they could rest easy. The Black Binding, with its creaky floors and towering shelves, was more than just a bookshop—it was their haven, a place where history came alive and where secrets were kept safe.

Before heading to bed, James paused at the entrance to the Bear Room, where they had found the secret entrance to Grandpa's office. He ran his fingers over a carved key symbol on the bookshelf, thinking about all that had happened and all that was to come. What else could they uncover? What other mysteries could they solve? What wrongs of the past could be righted? James felt a renewed sense of excitement inside him. The adventure wasn't over; it was just beginning.

"This is just the start." he whispered to himself. Then, with one last glance around the bookshop, he headed off to bed, ready for whatever the future might hold.

THE END